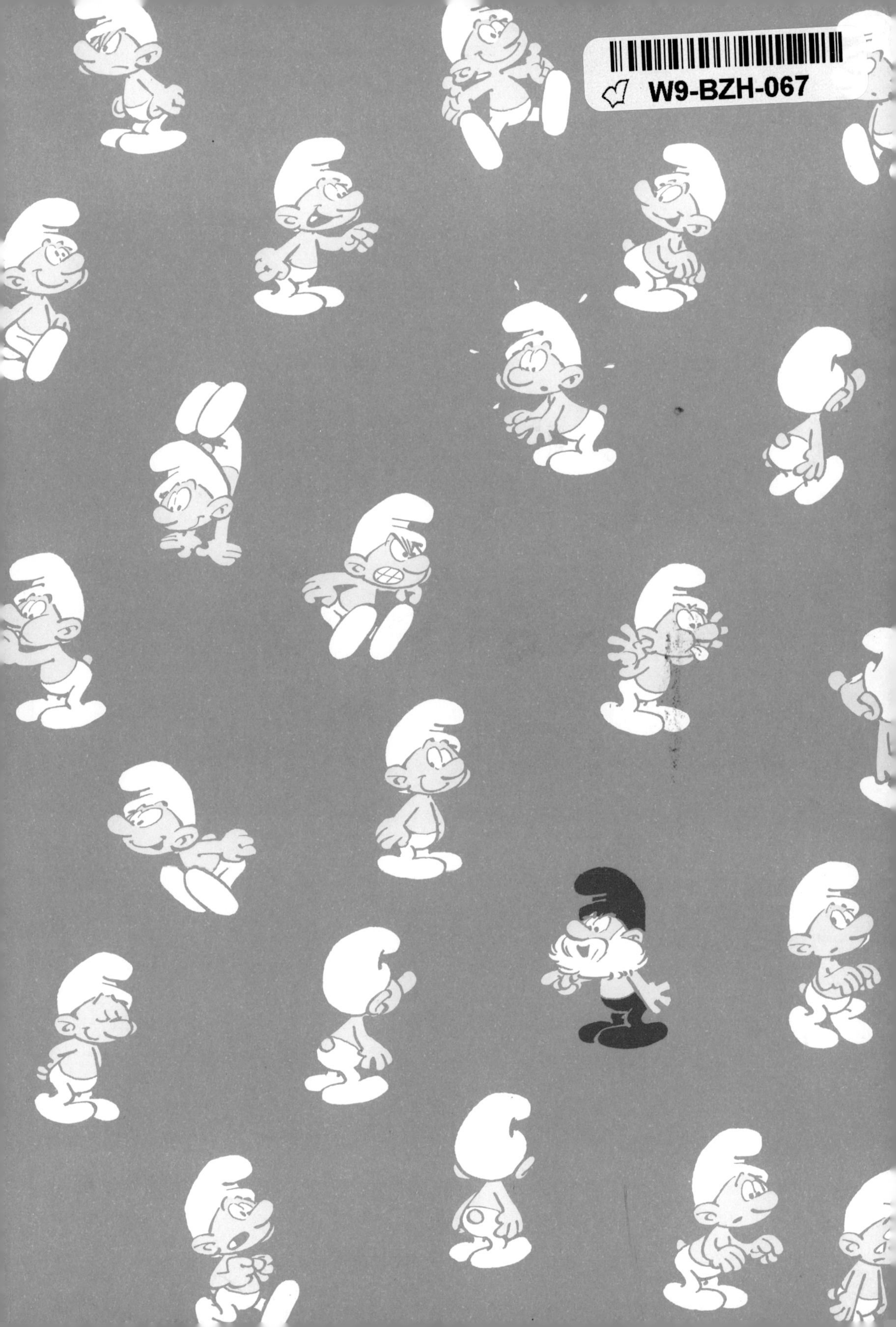

THE SMURFLINGS

Peyo

THE
SMURFLINGS

A **SMURFS** GRAPHIC NOVEL BY *Peyo*

PAPERCUTZ™

NEW YORK

SMURFS GRAPHIC NOVELS AVAILABLE FROM **PAPERCUTZ** ™

COMING SOON:

16. THE AEROSMURF

THE SMURFS graphic novels are available in paperback for $5.99 each and in hardcover for $10.99 each at booksellers everywhere. You can also order online at www.papercutz.com. Or call 1-800-886-1223, Monday through Fridays, 9 – 5 EST. MC, Visa, and AmEx accepted. To order by mail, please add $4.00 for postage and handling for first book ordered, $1.00 for each additional book and make check payable to NBM Publishing. Send to: Papercutz, 160 Broadway, Suite 700, East Wing, New York, NY 10038.

THE SMURFS graphic novels are also available digitally wherever e-books are sold.

WWW.PAPERCUTZ.COM

THE SMURFLINGS

© Peyo - 2013 - Licensed through Lafig Belgium - www.smurf.com

SCHTROUMPF SMURF SCHLUMPF I PUFFI PITUFO

English translation copyright © 2013 by Papercutz. All rights reserved.

"The Smurflings"
BY PEYO

"Puppy and the Smurfs"
BY PEYO

"The Smurfs and the Little Ghosts"
BY PEYO

"The Smurfs and the Booglooboo"
BY PEYO

Joe Johnson, SMURFLATIONS
Adam Grano, SMURFIC DESIGN
Janice Chiang, LETTERING SMURFETTE
Matt. Murray, SMURF CONSULTANT
Beth Scorzato, SMURF COORDINATOR
Michael Petranek, ASSOCIATE SMURF
Jim Salicrup, SMURF-IN-CHIEF

PAPERBACK EDITION ISBN: 978-1-59707-407-0
HARDCOVER EDITION ISBN: 978-1-59707-408-7

PRINTED IN CHINA FEBRUARY 2013 BY WKT CO. LTD.
3/F PHASE I LEADER INDUSTRIAL CENTRE
188 TEXACO ROAD, TSEUN WAN, N.T., HONG KONG

Papercutz books may be purchased for business or promotional use. For information on bulk purchases please contact Macmillan Corporate and Premium Sales Department at (800) 221-7945 x5442.

DISTRIBUTED BY MACMILLAN
FIRST PAPERCUTZ PRINTING

J
Peyo

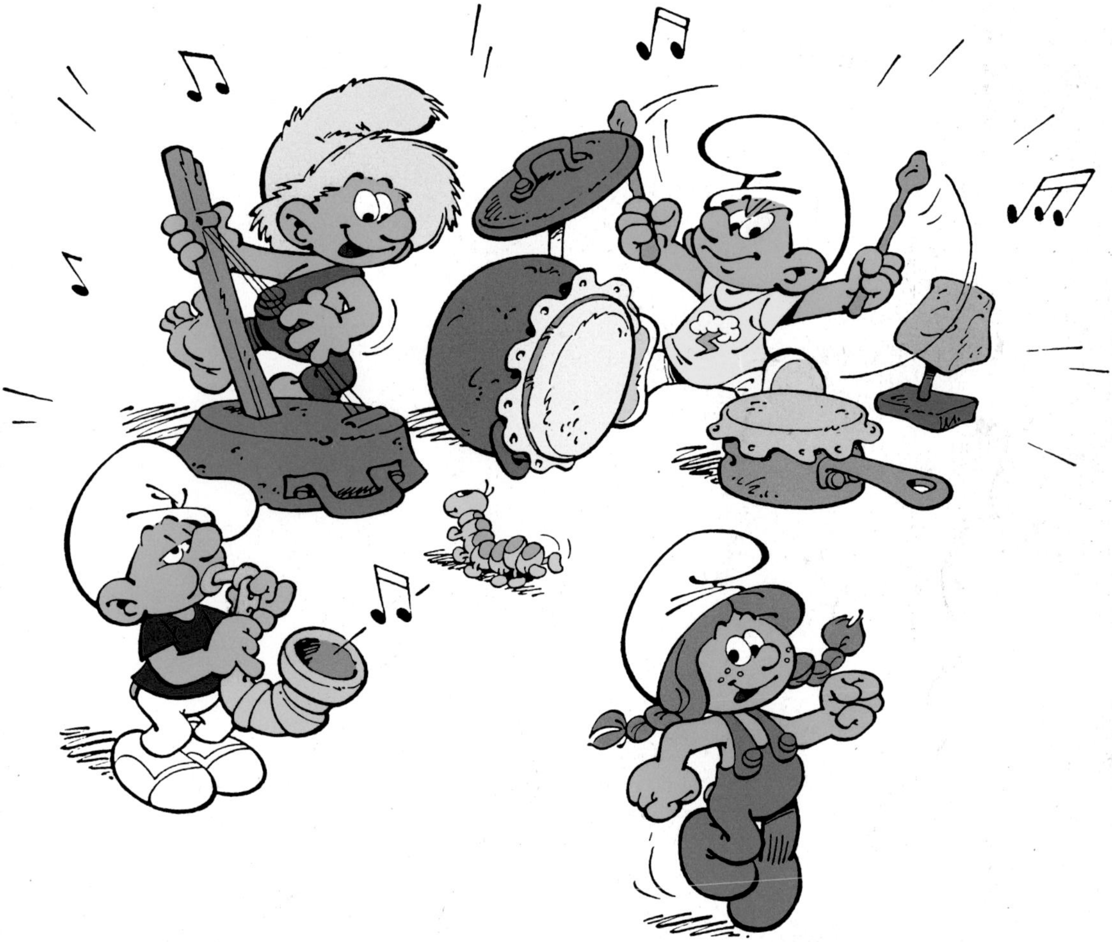

THE SMURFLINGS

Day is breaking over the Smurf Village. Like usual, the window of Papa Smurf's laboratory has remained lit all night long. Papa Smurf is working very, very hard...

...and two drops of smurfapirium smurfimus...

There! I carefully smurf everything...

And... wait exactly one sandglass before smurfing in the reagent!

Starting... NOW!

I must not make a smurfstake! A little too early or a little too late, and it all could be smurfed!

DZIM BOOM PWAAAAT

What the--?! MY SANDGLASS! BROKEN!

How much time's left? Five? Four? Three? Uh... Too bad, I'll pour! Two! One...

BOOOM

OOMPAOOMPAOOMPAHAAATEERELEEE TEERELEEE

...going on?

They've gone completely smurfers!

LABORATORY

!

DZIMBOOM TIROOM POOLILA PWAAATPWEEE DINGELINGELLONG

Ah! It's you, Papa Smurf!

What's all this ruckus? Are you crazy?

What's gotten into you-- making all this racket?

...what's... can't understand you!

ENOUGH!

WEOOEE...

What the smurf's got you smurfing music at this hour?

But, Papa Smurf, we're rehearsing! We're smurfing a big concert tonight! Remember?

Ah! Hmm! That's right! Uh, okay, continue!

Good! Let's take it from the top... Smurf, two, three...

Meanwhile, my experiment is ruined! And... I don't even have a sandglass left!

Hey! Snappy Smurf, Natural Smurf, and Slouchy Smurf! That gives me an idea!

Your butterfly's making me mad!

But Butterfly's nice!

Yep!

Peyo

2

Tell me, you three, are you smurfing anything at the moment?

Well...

Uh...

Actually...

Good! In that case, hurry off to Father Time's and ask him for a sandglass. Mine's broken!

We got tricked!

Bah! This'll smurf Butterfly a little exercise!

Yep!

Hm...? The Smurfette seems very sad!

Is something wrong, Smurfette?

Yes! Well, I... I'd really like to have a female friend!

Alas, there's only one Smurfette! And that's you!

I know! Too bad!

Is it far yet?

No! We're there! There's Father Time's home!

Oooo! It's spooky!

(∗) And not "tick-tock" (--Editor)

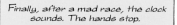

Panel 1:

Suddenly, the hands start spinning, turning faster and faster. And always in reverse...

DONG DING
TOCK
TICK TICK
TOCK TOCK
TOCK-TICK
DING

Panel 2:

Finally, after a mad race, the clock sounds. The hands stop.

BONG

Panel 3:

The door opens and...

GLIP

Panel 4:

What happened?

I don't know!

I feel all strange!

Panel 5:

That's funny! Our clothes have gotten too big!

No--I think we've become smaller,

And where's Butterfly?

Panel 6:

Hee hee hee! Butterfly! You've gotten younger, too! You've become a caterpillar again!

Panel 7:

All right! What do we do? Do we wait for Father Time so he can smurf us back to our normal size?

Why? Does it bother you being Smurflings?

No!

Panel 8:

Okay then, let's go back!

Panel 9:

Yes, but you're forgetting Papa Smurf's sandglass!

Bah! We'll take one and leave a note!

Panel 10:

I'm curious to see the other Smurfs' faces once they smurf us!

Hee hee hee! Me, too!

If they make smurf of us, I'm going to smurf mad!

...And once you smurfed out of the clock, you were little?

Well, yes! It's funny, isn't it?

Look at Butterfly!

And we didn't forsmurf your sandglass!

But this is a catasmurfphe! We have to smurf something! I'll search for an antidote.

And quick!

Good smurf of smurfs!

Come, come! Calm down! We think we're just smurf like this!

Well, yeah! You old folks are making a big fuss over nothing!

Old folks?! Say, my young friend, have a little respect for your elders! Back in my day...

No way! You're not going to start annoying us with your "back in my days"!

¿Grr!¿ I can tell I'm going to get mad!

And yet, he's right! It's certain that, back in my day...

Oh, no! Not you, too Papa Smurf! Your day was your day! Now we don't give a smurf about your day! We're living in the present, not the past!

Oh! Such language! Back in my day...

Yes! We'd never have allowed ourselves--!

Kids today!

Okay! We won't speak of it further! It's over! Agreed?

No way! I think Papa Smurf's right and, what's more, Papa Smurf is always right, and when Papa Smurf says that, back in his day...

¿sigh!¿

Hey! What are you...

AAAAAH

BOOM

That's curious! This they were already doing back in my day!

11

We don't need to be lectured, Papa Smurf, we need new clothes!

That's right! Hey! Smurf!

Yes?

Not you, Smurf! I said "Smurf" and not "Smurf"!

But I'm a Smurf!

Speaking Smurf isn't simple, eh?

Ah! There's Tailor Smurf!

Come here, Smurflings! I'll smurf you some cute, little clothes!

Two apples and a half! This Smurfling's a tall one!

Hey, don't smurf us any stupid, "classic" outfits, eh? A little imagination, eh!

Imagination? But...

Wait! We'll show you what we want! Smurf me those scissors!

But...

I'm curious to smurf what Tailor's making for the Smurflings!

Ah! It's you, Vanity Smurf! So what do you think of them?

AAAH!

What?!

Smelling salts! Quick! Smelling salts!

It's... it's a nightmare!

In the end, the Smurflings are soon adopted by all the Smurfs...

So, how's it smurfing, Smurflings?

It's smurfing fine!

Hey! I'm going to smurf you a nice cake! For this evening!

That's a smurf idea!

My goodness, your caterpillar is smurf!

They look smurf, dressed like that!

Yes, eh? You know this is Butterfly?

Well, by almost all...

WELL, ME, I DON'T LIKE GROWN-UP SMURFS!

But, I didn't say anything!

No! But you thought it, Grouchy Smurf!

How did he guess?

Me, I don't like Smurflings!

Hey! Smurflings! Here's a gift for you!

Oh?

Another of your notorious gifts that smurfs up in your face once you open it?

Yes! Hee hee hee! Open it fast!

Very funny! But, still, don't think we're smurf just because we're little, Jokey Smurf!

13

TONIGHT

Grand Smurfonic Concert

under the direction of Brainy Smurf

Aw, darn! I'd forgotten!

And did you see who's going to smurf the orchestra?

Yeah! It won't be a very smurf evening!

Wait! I think I have an idea! Smurf closely...

Hee hee hee! That's a good idea!

But where will we find that?

I think I know. Come on!

Hey! Handy Smurf! Could you smurf us three musical instruments for this evening?

For this evening?!

Well, I don't know! Go smurf in the shed and see if there's something that'll do the job!

Great! There's some of everything in here!

Hey! I think I've found what I needed!

Me, too!

And me, three! Now to work!

?

KLANK BING DZIIIIII CLITOC TOG

Oh, hey!
Papa Smurf!

We'd like to
play tonight, too!
Can we?

Look!
We have
everything
we need!

Say
yes!

Well, uh...
it's just... Oh! And
then, after all,
why not?

YIPPEE!

We have just
enough time to
practice some
harmonizing!

I like it when
youngsters smurf
the initiative!

Start
without me!
I'm going to
drop by Poet
Smurf's!

You wouldn't
have a little
glue?

Well, yes!

TONIGHT

Grand
Smurfonic
Conce

With the group
«THE SMURFLINGS»

under the ...tion of
Br...ny Smurf

Papa Smurf! Papa Smurf!
Did you see? The Smurflings
want to smurf music, too!

So what? That's their right!
In the land of the Smurfs,
everyone is free to smurf
as he likes!

Fine! Fine! Let them
smurf! But we'll see who gets
the last smurf!

Peyo

15

And that evening...

TIMBOOBAHTIMBOOBATDRAGOOTIMBOOBATABOOGROOTTIMBOOBAGLOPGOOGAMGLOPERUTOTIMBOOBA

TIMBOOBAGROOT
TIMBOOBAGOOGAM
TIMBOOBAGORAK

Mezzo vivace, allegro ma non troppo!

SNRRK! ZZZZ!

Lazy Smurf! Wake up! You're snoring!

Huh? What?! But I'm not Lazy Smurf!

Oh? Sorry...

TIMMM BOOO BAAHH

Voila! That'll bring the house down with applause!

!?

CLAP CLAP CLAP

Hmm... And now for something in a different style: meet **THE SMURFLINGS!**

Why, yes! Go ahead, kids! The tomatoes will soon be smurfing! Hee hee hee!

One... two... one-two-three-four...

WAHHWOOTHRUMMTHRUMMBLAMBLAM

Hey!

Wow! That music's smurf!

What rhythm!

Smurftastic!

Yes, that's smurfily good!

No, it's bad! It's the music of savages! Smurf tomatoes at them!

SPLATCH

Come on, Smurfs! Let's leave with dignity!

Wait! We like what they're doing!

TEEPAPALALA DEPALALEEDA

♪ COME ON, SMURFS, DANCE! ♫

LEELALEEDALEELADOO

GUHDOOGUHDOO DZINK

BIMBALA BIM BAM BOOM

BIMBALA BIM BAM BOOM

Me, I don't like bimbala bim bam booms!

Brainy Smurf? He went that way!

Okay, traditions are all very nice, but you have to get with the times... stay young.

Uh... maybe you're right...

Why, of course...! All right, goodnight, Brainy Smurf!

♪ TATATA DZIM BOOM, YEAH! ♫

Peyo

12

The next morning...

SNNURK ZZZZ!

Hey! Wake up! The sun's up!

Hmmm...?

6!

YAWN! What an evening! I'm sleepsmurfing!

Hold on... The Smurfette! She looks unhappy.

Hey, Smurfette! You look really sad!

We didn't see you last night!

That's right! How come?

I'm sorry, but I didn't feel up to having fun!

For some time, I've been dreaming of having a girl friend! You all have guy friends! I don't have a girl friend!

But alas, there's only one Smurfette! So, I feel a little lonely...

A girl friend...

What could we do?

I don't know!

Hey! I have an idea! But let's go see Papa Smurf first!

?

?

13

18

Yes, the Smurfette was originally a creation by Gargamel!/* Why?

Oh! No reason!

Nothing!

Uh, do you smurf the formula that he used?

No, in fact!

Ah?

Okay!

Too bad!

Understood! Move out! To Gargamel's!

Here, Azrael! ⊙∿⊙ ☼! You stink, you-- fleabag!

MEOOOW!

I took one five years ago! Now, you're going to take A BATH!

HEY! GET BACK HERE, YOU DIRTY BEAST!

WHIIIIISSSS

Come here or I'll change you into... **INTO A DOG!**

He's gone!

Let's go! Let's camosmurf ourselves--to be safe!

Good! And now we must smurf that famous formula!

(*) See THE SMURFS #4 "The Smurfette"

19

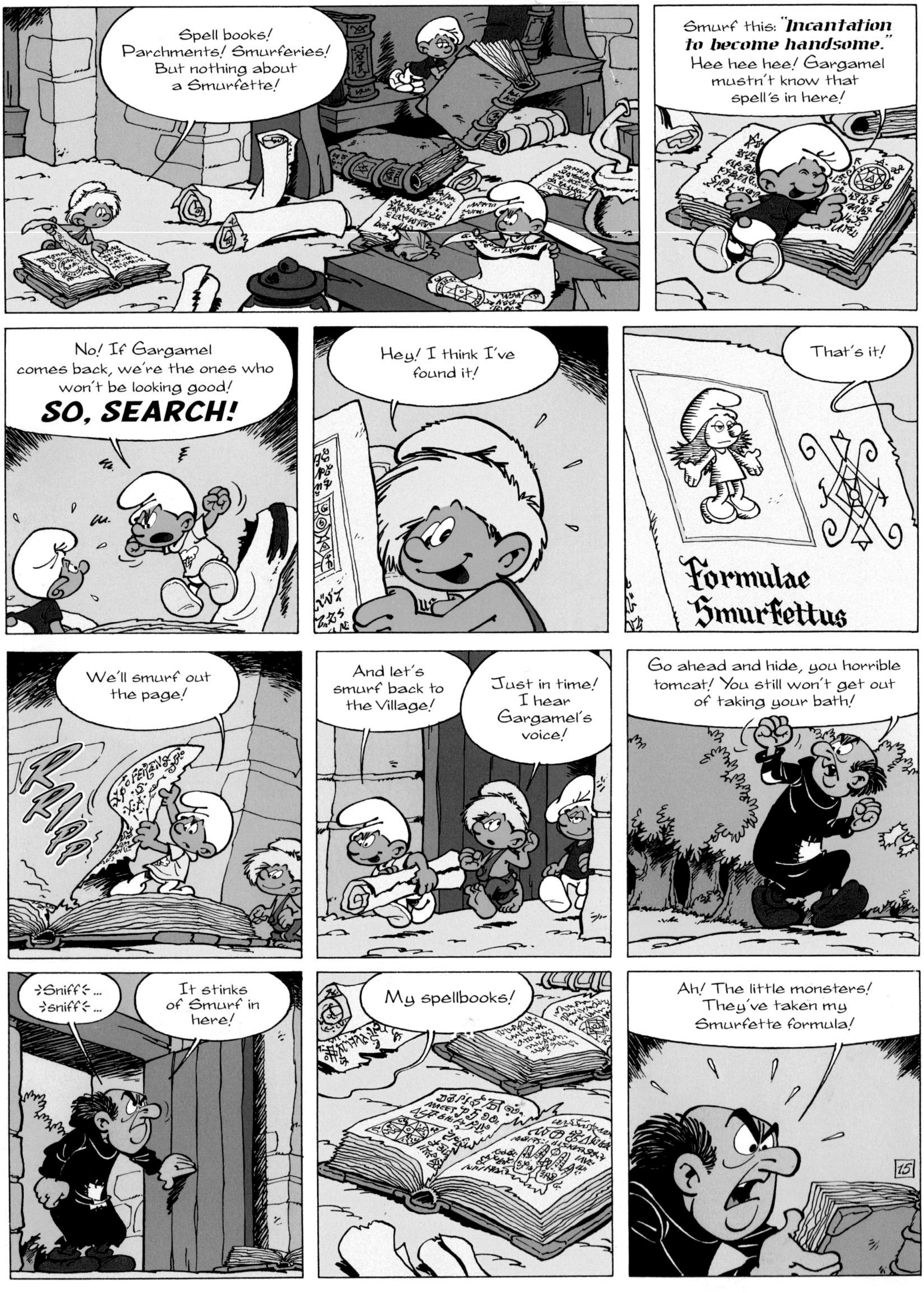
Spell books! Parchments! Smurferies! But nothing about a Smurfette!
Smurf this: "Incantation to become handsome." Hee hee hee! Gargamel mustn't know that spell's in here!
No! If Gargamel comes back, we're the ones who won't be looking good! SO, SEARCH!
Hey! I think I've found it!
That's it!
Formulae Smurfettus
We'll smurf out the page!
RRIPP
And let's smurf back to the Village!
Just in time! I hear Gargamel's voice!
Go ahead and hide, you horrible tomcat! You still won't get out of taking your bath!
Sniff ... *sniff* ...
It stinks of Smurf in here!
My spellbooks!
Ah! The little monsters! They've taken my Smurfette formula!
15

If they want to make another one, they'll need blue clay!

But there exists only one place where one can find that kind of soil...

And that's in the cave of the Source! HA! HA! HA! I have to get there before they do!

In the meantime, the Smurflings have returned to the Village...

Okay! We'll smurf all these ingredients in Papa Smurf's laboratory! But...

But I've never seen blue clay in there...

Let's go ask him where we can find some!

In the cave of the Source! Why?

Oh! Just curious!

Yeah!

Thanks, Papa Smurf!

That's bizarre! I wonder what those three are busy smurfing? Are they going to go into the cave?

But someone's already there...

Quick! Throw the spell!

ABRACADASPROOTCH DZEEMERLI TOCK!

And voila! Now any bit of this clay exposed to the noon-day sun will **EXPLODE!** Ha! Ha! Ha!

16

Let the Smurfs come! They'll get a surprise! Ha! Ha! Ha! Okay! Now I must find Azrael and make him take **A BATH.**

Ah! We're there!

AZRAEL! WHERE ARE YOU?

!

Meeoow...

?

Shhhh!

!?!?

So, there's that famous blue clay! Let's smurf some quick and go back!

Later, at the Village, night has fallen...

Well? Did you smurf the cave?

The cave?

Ah, yes! The cave!

What cave?

I'm certain they're smurfing something from me... Hmm!

Goodnight, Smurflings!

Goodnight, Papa Smurf!

SSNOOOOOZZZZZZZ

All right! All the Smurfs are sound asmurf! We can go!

LABORATORY

‧Whew!‧ It's open!

Now to work! We have to smurf a fire...

Shape the clay...

Find the right ingredients...

First, fill a basin halfway with water!

Here are all the bottles I smurfed!

How's your modeling smurfing?

Well, it's not easy!

...And the Smurf'lings work all night long...

I have some white thread!

Good!

Here's the candle!

‧Snnrr‧ ZZZZ...

Z₃₃

Is the mixture ready?

Yes! We can't smurf it on the fire!

Get smurfing! It'll smurf dawn soon!

Yikes! Pull the basin off! It's boiling! And it mustn't boil!

‧Koff koff‧...

BLUB BURBLEBURBLE BLUB

‧Whew!‧ The smoke's dissipating! I'm curious to see whether—

18

Hello!

Oh!

Eh!

Hmm...

23

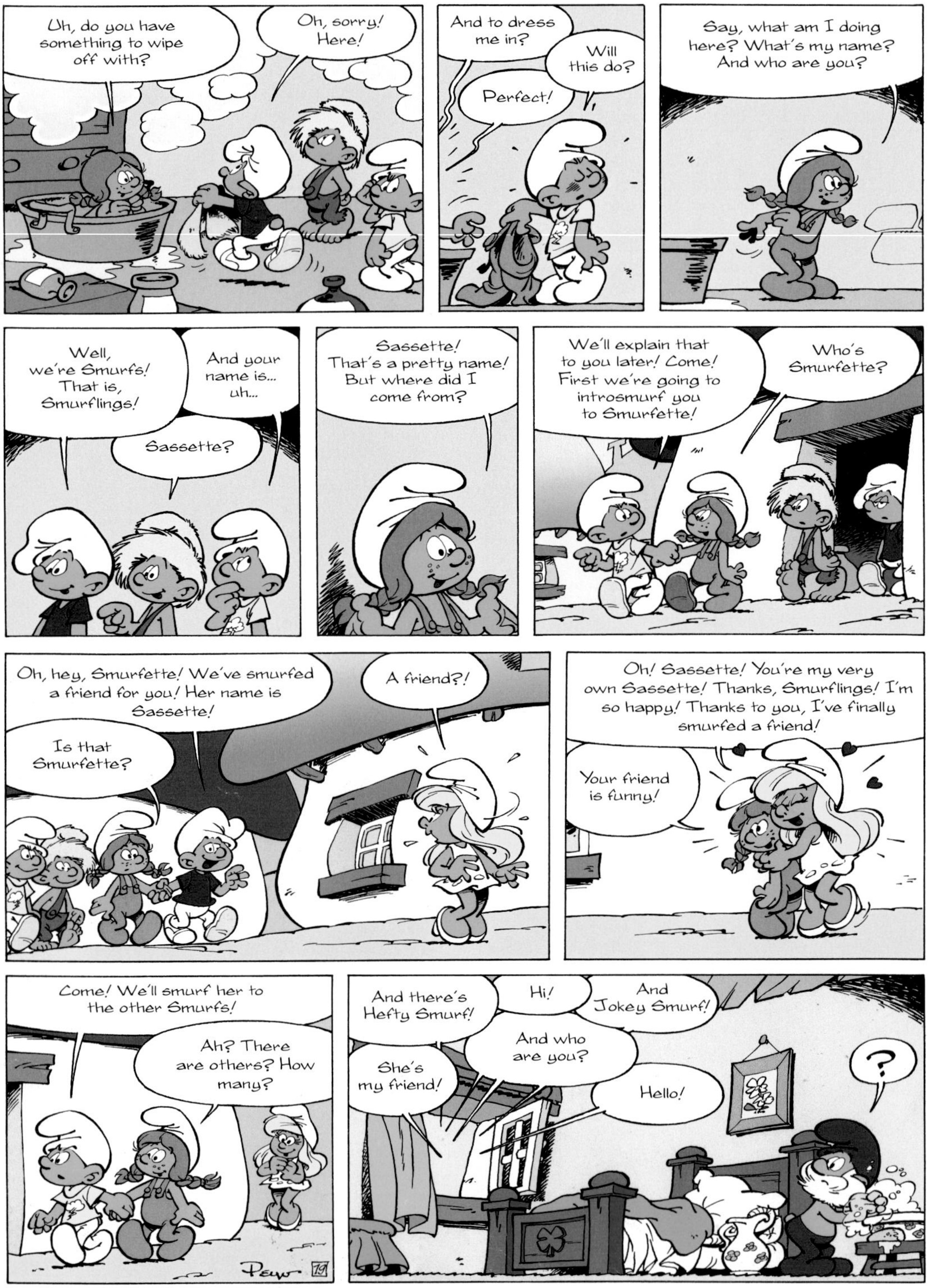
Uh, do you have something to wipe off with?
Oh, sorry! Here!
And to dress me in?
Will this do?
Perfect!
Say, what am I doing here? What's my name? And who are you?
Well, we're Smurfs! That is, Smurflings!
And your name is... uh...
Sassette?
Sassette! That's a pretty name! But where did I come from?
We'll explain that to you later! Come! First we're going to introsmurf you to Smurfette!
Who's Smurfette?
Oh, hey, Smurfette! We've smurfed a friend for you! Her name is Sassette!
A friend?!
Is that Smurfette?
Oh! Sassette! You're my very own Sassette! Thanks, Smurflings! I'm so happy! Thanks to you, I've finally smurfed a friend!
Your friend is funny!
Come! We'll smurf her to the other Smurfs!
Ah? There are others? How many?
Peyo
19
And there's Hefty Smurf!
Hi!
And Jokey Smurf!
She's my friend!
And who are you?
Hello!
?

And here's Papa Smurf!

This is Sassette! My friend!

Hello, Sassette! Where are you from?

Oh! He's old!

I don't know anything! Who am I...? What am I smurfing here? Why? How? Nobody's telling me anything!

Hmm... before answering you, I'd like to smurf the Smurflings a few questions!

Come, Sassette! I'll smurf you to my house!

Well?

Uh...

Hmm...

So...

Smurfette wanted a girl friend! So, we wanted to smurf one for her and we smurfed a formula from Gargamel's!

GARGAMEL'S!

And where is that formula?

In your laboratory.

And who allowed you to smurf in my laboratory, eh?

NO SMURFING

Tell me... Do you still have any blue clay left?

A little!

Good! I'm going to analyze it! I hope for your sakes I don't find anything abnormal about it!

Can we help you?

No! Smurf home and stay there! You're grounded!

LABORATORY

SMURFING

Peyo

25

While you're smurfing a cup of smurf, I'm going to take a smurf around the Village!

Don't go too far!

TRALALALA LALA...

!

Oh, you're the Grouchy Smurf!

Hmm...

Why are you grouchy? Is that your nature? Were you born like that? Hey, I'm smurfing you a question.

Me, I don't like questions!

And I smurf you don't like smurfettes!

Me, I don't like smurfettes!

Why not?

Because they're creatures from Gargamel! And I don't like Gargamel!

Who's Gargamel?

He's a wicked sorcerer!

Oh? And where does he live?

In a hovel on the other side of the forest!

Oh?

And stop smurfing me questions! I don't like being smurfed questions!

On the other side of the forest... Well, well...

TRALEELALEE LALA

Apparently I don't see anything abnormal! I'll try light beams!

Let's see... this is the equivalent of a sunbeam's intensity at noon...

BOOOM

For smurf's sake! At noon, Sassette's going to **EXPLODE!**

Papa Smurf, what happened?

You're not wounded?

I'm okay! Where's Sassette?

ATORY

She's no longer here! I don't think I ought to have smurfed her about Gargamel and his hovel, because she went off in that direction! And I don't like that!

!!

WHAAT?! MY SASSETTE!

You stupid smurf!

POW BAM SOK

Me, I don't like SOKs!

Go look for her quick! I must find the antidote before noon! I'll rejoin you!

Ah! I think it's here!

?

NOK NOK NOK

Are you Gargamel? Hello! My name is Sassette and I have a few questions to ask you!

AAAH!

27

Go away, you wretch! It's almost noon!

So what? Why must I go away because it'll soon be noon? Eh? Say? Is there some reason?

Don't stay here! Go back to your cursed Smurfs!

But why?

Meanwhile...

Smurfreka! I've smurfed the antidote!

Quick! Resmurf the other Smurfs before it's too late!

SASSETTE!

YOO-HOO!

Who--? The Smurfs!

HEY! HERE I AM!

SASSETTE!

You're alive!

Well, yes! Why not?

My Sassette? My friend!

We were asmurfed we'd never see you again!

Oh, really?

Yikes! The sun! It's at its zenith! She's going to exsmurf!

RUN FOR YOUR SMURFS!

Why are you all smurfing away now? What did I do? I don't undersmurf anything anymore!

SPLAAT

23

♪Whew!♪ Saved! In the nick of time!

But, is anyone ever going to explain to me what's smurfing?

Later! Let's smurf back to the Village! Gargamel mustn't be far away!

Later! Always later!

That's strange! It's noon, and I haven't heard their Sassette explode!

Was I mistaken in my spells? Let's see, let's see...

SCRATCH SCRATCH

This isn't normal! A noon-time sunbeam and...

BOOOM

!

BAM

AZRAEL!

Meeoow?

I have to get revenge on someone! And it'll be on you! You're going to take that bath! Ha! Ha! Ha!

So that's the whole story, Sassette!

And you're my friend now!

♪We're going to have a little party!♪

Okay, Smurflings, you're not grounded, but...

DON'T DO IT AGAIN!

THE END

29

PUPPY AND THE SMURFS

One evening, at the Smurf Village...

...and the awful dragon smurfed toward the princess!

And then?

And then?

The handsome prince arrived and he smurfed the dragon. And there! It's late now, you must go and smurf to bed.

Whew! Goodnight, Papa Smurf!

Those stories scare me!

Why do you listen to them, then?

Because I like feeling scared!

GRAAOOOW!

Yeah, that's Jokey Smurf!

BOOO!

Very good, that's very scary! Bye, Jokey Smurf!

'Night!

Peyo

They're harder and harder to scare...!

Maybe...I'm no longer up to the job...

sigh...

1

I know full well those dragon tales are just stories, but still...!

GRRR...

AWOOOoo

Papa Smuu-uurf!

It's a stressful night...

It-- it sounds like a monster's cry... But like Papa Smurf says, monsters don't really exist... So he says!

My blood is smurfing cold!

Me, I don't like woof-woofs!

Maybe it's Jokey Smurf again!

WOOF WOOF!

But the next morning, everything seems back to normal. The Village awakens.

ZZZ

WAAAAAH!

What a night! What stupid dreams a Smurf can smurf!

AHHH!

A MONSTER!

Where?

THERE!

We have to smurf it before it destroys the whole village!

And before it eats us!

Quick! Some ropes! A net!

Watch out! Maybe it bites!

Or spits fire!

Look out! It's waking up!

Be careful!

Peyo 2

Hey! It's Puppy!

Puppy?

?

That's a good Puppy! But what's got you smurfing here?

WOOFF! WOOFF!

You know this beast, Papa Smurf?

Of course! It's the Enchanter Homnibus' dog!(1)

HEY LOOK!

He's smurfing a medallion around his neck. Maybe there's a message inside?

Wait! I'll open it!

WHOA!

Smurfin' Smurfs! I smurfed something like a shock!

Wait! I'll open it!

WAHOOAAAH!

Clumsy! Let me do it!

Eeeee!

Your turn!

Well, uh...

No! Not you, Baby! It's dangerous!

Arhooooo!

Uhh... okay! I'm going to smurf a message to Homnibus telling him his dog is here! In the meantime, we'll care of him!

Come, Puppy!

3

(1) See THE SMURFS #2 "The Smurfs and the Magic Flute"

32

And return quickly with the response!

Ah! I'm happy to see they've adopted Puppy!

Smurf the bally!

You don't say "bally," you say "ball"!

You go, doggy!

You don't say "doggy," you say "dog."

Hey, Puppy! Here's something yummy!

You don't say "something yummy," you say "food."

Who's going to take a bubble-bath?

You don't say a "bubble-bath," you say a "bath"!

That evening...

No, Puppy! Not in the bed! In the doghouse!

You don't say "in the doghouse," you say "in the doggy..." uh... no, sorry!

The next morning...

COCKADOOD! WOOF WOOF!

Look! My messenger's back! I'm curious to see what Homnibus has to say!

Why... it's my message! Homnibus must be away from home! The best thing would be to take Puppy back to him! Let's go, Smurfs!

Oh!

Already?

4

33

Is it far, Papa Smurf?

No! We're almost at Homnibus's home!

I hope he's there and can reveal to us the secret of Puppy's medallion!

It's the Smurfs! Do you hear what they're saying, Azrael? Let's follow them!

Homnibus!

The Smurfs! Puppy! Come in!

I was worried! Yesterday, he ran off, and I searched everywhere for him, but to no avail! I just now got back!

Hey! Papa Smurf! The medallion!

Ah, yes, the medallion! We tried to open it, but with no success!

We all tried!

Me, too! The old mage who gave me Puppy told me that whoever succeeded in opening it would become his master.

And that Puppy would do everything he was ordered to do...!

Heh heh!

Azrael, we must have that dog! Come! I have a plan!

If you really like him, I'll happily give him to you. He could protect you, perhaps, in case of danger!

YIPPEE!

Oh, yes, Papa Smurf!

Great!

Goodbye, Homnibus! And thanks!

Come, Puppy!

34

We'll have to smurf him a good education, teach him to act right, to obey, to fetch what we smurf for him, to eat right, to not slobber, nor lick, to be a good guard dog...

Poor beast!

MEEEOOOWWW..

AZRAEL!

PUPPY! COME BACK!

WOOF! WOOF!

!

HA! HA! I've got you!

It's awful! Puppy is Gargamel's prisoner! He's going to kill him!

No! Look! I think he's going to try to open his medallion!

Exactly! In that case, we no longer have anything to fear for Puppy! Let's go home!

And now, I'm going to open your medallion and I'll be your master! HA! HA! HA!

YIII!!

DIRTY DOG!

Follow him! He'll lead us to the Smurf Village, and then we'll capture all of them!

Ah! There's Puppy! You see-- nothing happened to him!
WOOF! WOOF!
HA! HA! HA!
Heavens! GARGAMEL!
I knew I'd arrive in the Smurf Village by following that dog!
Run for your smurfs!
I'll get you all!
WOOF!
SSSSSSSSSSSSS
Run, Puppy!
YIII! YIII! YIII!
YIII!
No afraid, Puppy!
Baby open medal!
TCHING
TCHIIING
TCHING
TCHHIIING
Look! Baby has opened the medallion! He's the Puppy's master!
Another one!
HELP!
GARGAMEL! Bad! Bing, Puppy! POW!
GRRR!
Peyo
7

GRRR!

What does that filthy beast want with me...? Get! **DOWN!**

OWWW!

Bite, puppy!

SAVED! That's a good mean doggy!

You don't say...

CHOMP

Oww!

YIPPEE!

You go, Puppy! Smurf him!

OUCH! OUCH! OUCH!

Me, I really like mean dogs!

HURRAY FOR BABY!

HURRAY FOR PUPPY!

Stay there, Azrael! I'm going to make you a medallion! And I'll be your master! At least, I hope so...!

BING BING

8

END

Peyo

THE SMURFS AND THE LITTLE GHOSTS

Look, Azrael, there are the abbey's ruins! They're haunted by little ghosts!

Hey! Want to play hide-and-seek?

Okay!

Hee! Hee!

There's nothing like a BIG ghost to frighten little ones! Hee! Hee! Hee!

Let's go, Azrael.

BOOOOO

OO

Eeeeek!

MEOW

?

Leave and never come back or I'll take you to the Land of Shadows!

BOOOBOOOOOOO...

Help! A demon!

AAMEE!

MEOW

Eeee! Let's get out of here!

MEOW GRR?

FFFT FFFT

Ha! Ha! Ha! It worked! I'll be able to look peacefully for the treasure that the monks hid here!

© Peyo

Follow me! We'll hide in the forest!

MRRAAAOW

AUROO!

Whatever you do, don't get wet, Azrael, otherwise the black color won't stick!

NEOW

GRR?

Whew! The little demon has stopped chasing us!

I was really afraid!

A little later...

Uh... I think we're lost!

?

There's a little path over here! That should lead us somewhere!

At that very moment...

Ha! Ha! Ha! I really got you, Brainy Smurf! What a good gag, eh? Hee, hee!

BLAM

BLAM

BLAM

It's completely stupid!

Me, I hate gifts!

© Peyo

Idiot! Nobody smurfs at your bad jokes, Jokey Smurf!

What? Oh, come on, it's just for laughs.

Hmm! Maybe he's right. I'll have to smurf up a new gag, but what?

2

The Weather Smurf said it won't rain tonight! I can leave my sheets outside to smurf!

?

Ha ha! I've got an idea! We'll see whether or not anyone smurfs at my jokes! Hee! Hee! Hee!

I'm going to scare them disguised as a smurf-ghost! Hee! Hee! Hee!

I'm going to smurf around the village in order to surprise the Smurfette! Hee, hee, hee!

?

!

Did you see that? It's a ghost like us!

Maybe it's a village of ghosts! Can we go see?

Yes, but let's be careful!

It's late. I'm glad I'm smurfing home!

BOOO!

Ha! Ha! Ha! It works! Boo! Boo!

HELP! A GHOST!

Hey, that's the Smurfette's voice!

BOOO! AHHHH!

A ghost! Help! AHHHHH!

Ha! Ha! Ha! It's too funny! I'm really enjoying myself Boo! Boo! Boo!

© Peyo

3

40

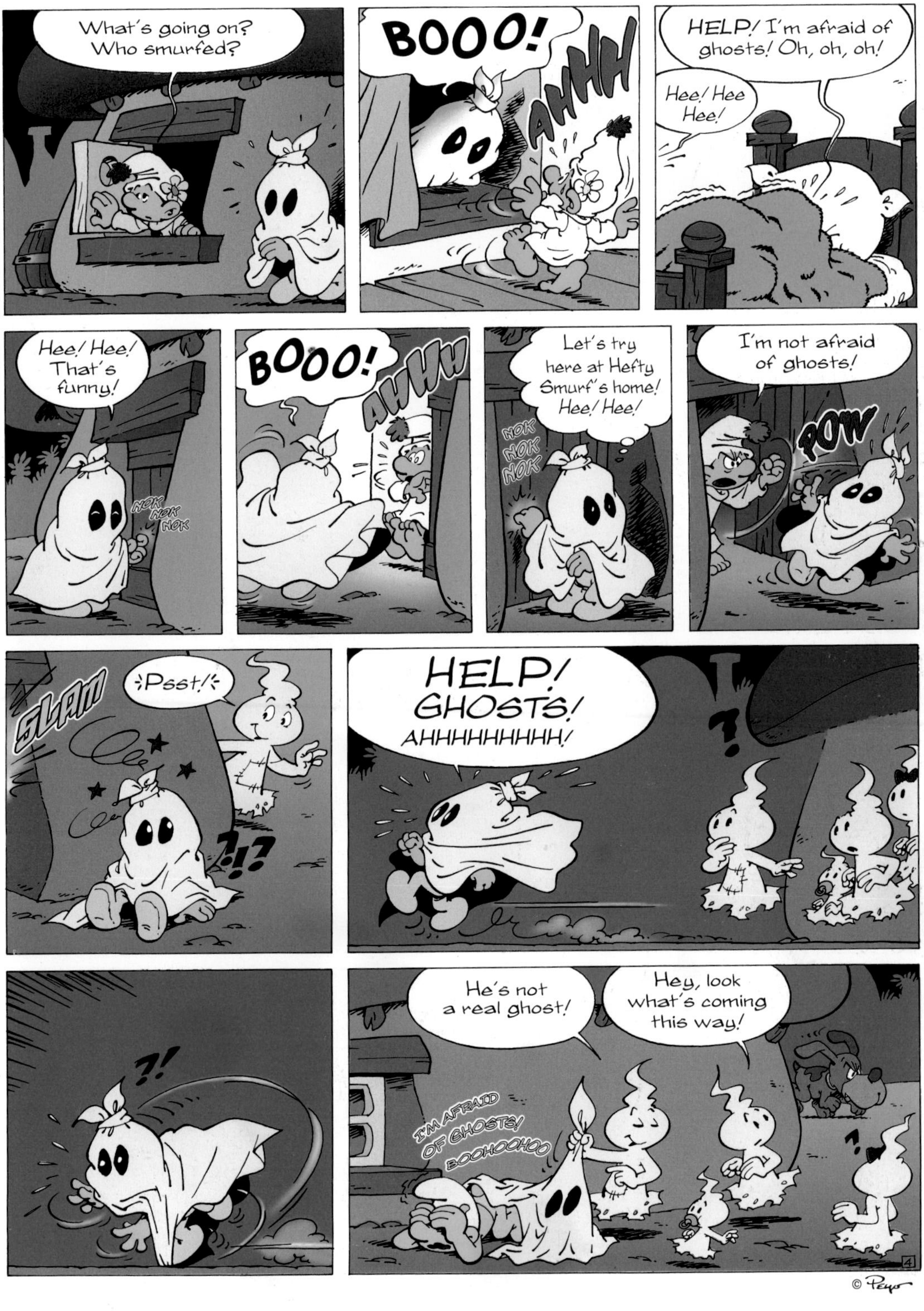
What's going on? Who smurfed?
BOOO!
AHHH
HELP! I'm afraid of ghosts! Oh, oh, oh!
Hee! Hee Hee!
Hee! Hee! That's funny!
NOK NOK NOK
BOOO!
AHHH
Let's try here at Hefty Smurf's home! Hee! Hee!
NOK NOK NOK
I'm not afraid of ghosts!
POW
SLAM
Psst!
?!?
HELP! GHOSTS! AHHHHHHHHH!
?
?!
He's not a real ghost!
Hey, look what's coming this way!
I'M AFRAID OF GHOSTS! BOOHOOHOO
?
4

What's all this ruckus, for smurf's sake?

LABORATORY

?

What's wrong, Papa Smurf?

There!

Calm down, Puppy! Those ghosts don't look very mean!

We're afraid of the big demon with paws!

Don't be afraid! He's our good dog, Puppy! He just doesn't know you! Who are you?

We're the little ghosts from the abbey! A big, mean, black demon with a skeleton head chased us out of the ruins that we usually haunt!

A demon with a smurf head?

?

This business worries me. We'll help you! Tomorrow, we'll smurf there and get acquainted with the facts of the matter.

Thank you, Papa Smurf!

The next morning...

Really, Smurfette, we're not smurfing for Halloween!

I thought of these little costumes of little monsters to scare the smurf out of the demon with a skeleton head!

We're scary!

Me, I hate monsters!

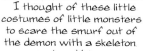

There it is!

Shh! Listen to those noises!

42

Stay hidden here. I'm going to go take a smurf in the ruins!

Be careful!

GRMBLLLSAKES! # * * 🌀!💢👁 I'll find that treasure! I want it!

For smurf's sake! It's Gargamel!

MEOW GRRRRR PFFST PFFFF

!?

Papa Smurf! That's better than any treasure! Hee! Hee!

Help!

MEOW!

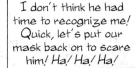

I don't think he had time to recognize me! Quick, let's put our mask back on to scare him! Ha! Ha! Ha!

Catch him, Azrael!

Azrael? I figured as much!

MEOW

Let's save Papa Smurf! ATTACK!

YAAAA

BOOO

GR!

!?!

MEOW

GRRN

‹Whew!›

MONSTERS! The ghosts have brought back the spirits of the forest!

YAAAA

BOOO

WOOF WOOF WOOF

YAAAA

MEOW

© Peyo

Quick, Azrael! Let's take shelter up here!

WOOF WOOF WOOF BOOOOO YAAAA

MEOW

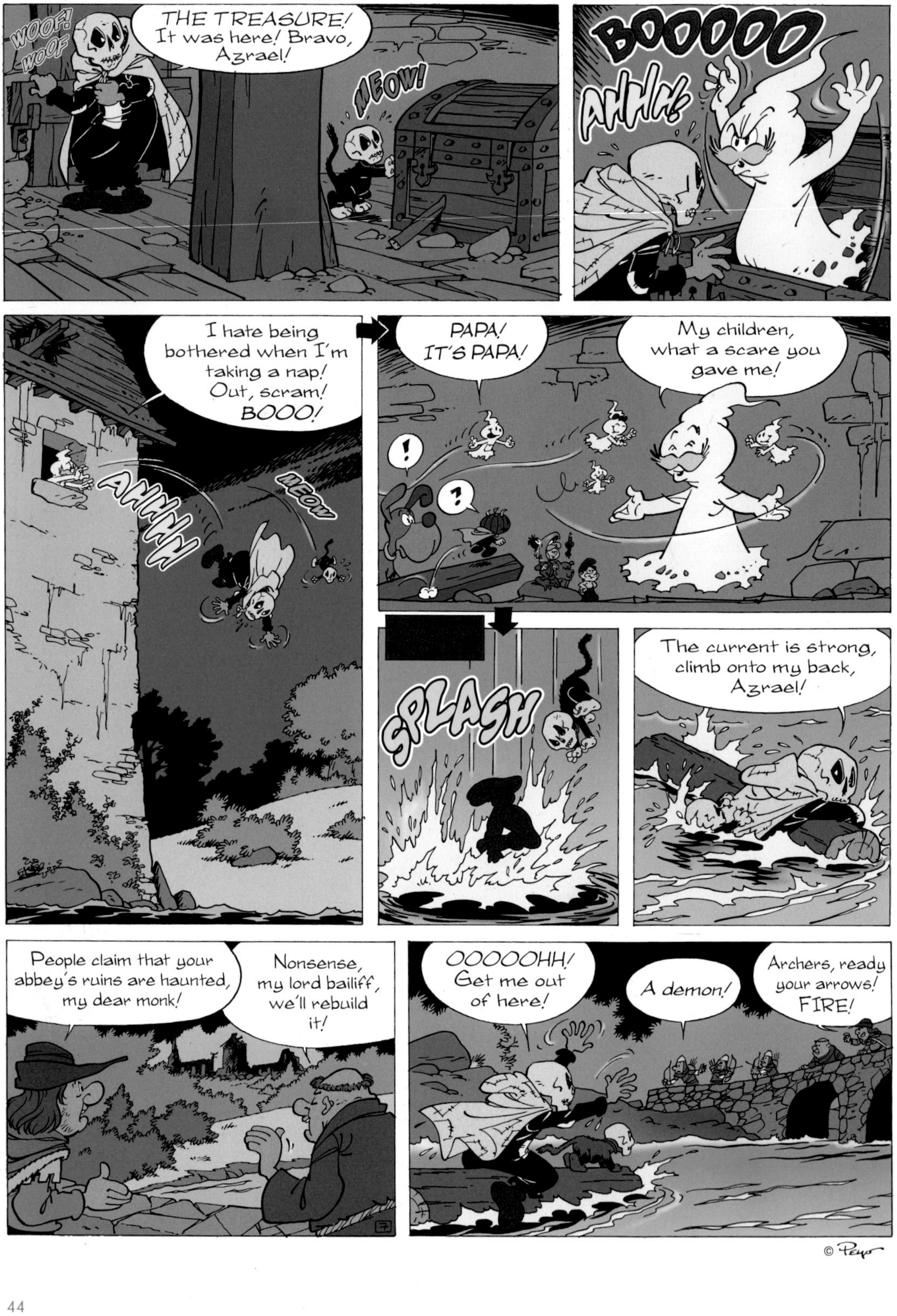
WOOF! WOOF
THE TREASURE! It was here! Bravo, Azrael!
MEOW!
BOOOOO
AHHHH!
I hate being bothered when I'm taking a nap! Out, scram! BOOO!
AHHHH
MEOW
PAPA! IT'S PAPA!
My children, what a scare you gave me!
!
?
[redacted]
SPLASH
The current is strong, climb onto my back, Azrael!
People claim that your abbey's ruins are haunted, my dear monk!
Nonsense, my lord bailiff, we'll rebuild it!
OOOOOHH! Get me out of here!
A demon!
Archers, ready your arrows! FIRE!

Let's flee! The baillif doesn't like sorcerers or demons!

OWW!

We captured them, sir!

No funny business! I'm not afraid of you demons!

!?!?

We must set an example! Tie those two jokers in the branches of that apple tree and forget about them!

Amen!

The baillif's soldiers are smurfing this way!

Follow me with your little ghosts. I know a place you can haunt in complete safety!

That old tower has been abandoned for ages! You can smurf there in peace!

Thank you, Papa Smurf!

HURRAH!

It's our new home, baby!

BOOO

It's time to smurf back to the village!

Good luck!

Goodbye! BOOOOOOOO

Hee, hee, the Baillif has smurfed Gargamel in the branches of the apple tree!

Get out of here! I'm a demon! ARHH ARHH!

SPLOTCH

SPLAT

RIGHT SMACK ON HIS SMURF!

HEE! HEE! HEE! HA! HA! HA!

SPLAT

Cursed Smurfs! You'll pay for that a hundred-fold!

ARHHHHH!

© Peyo ®

THE END.

45

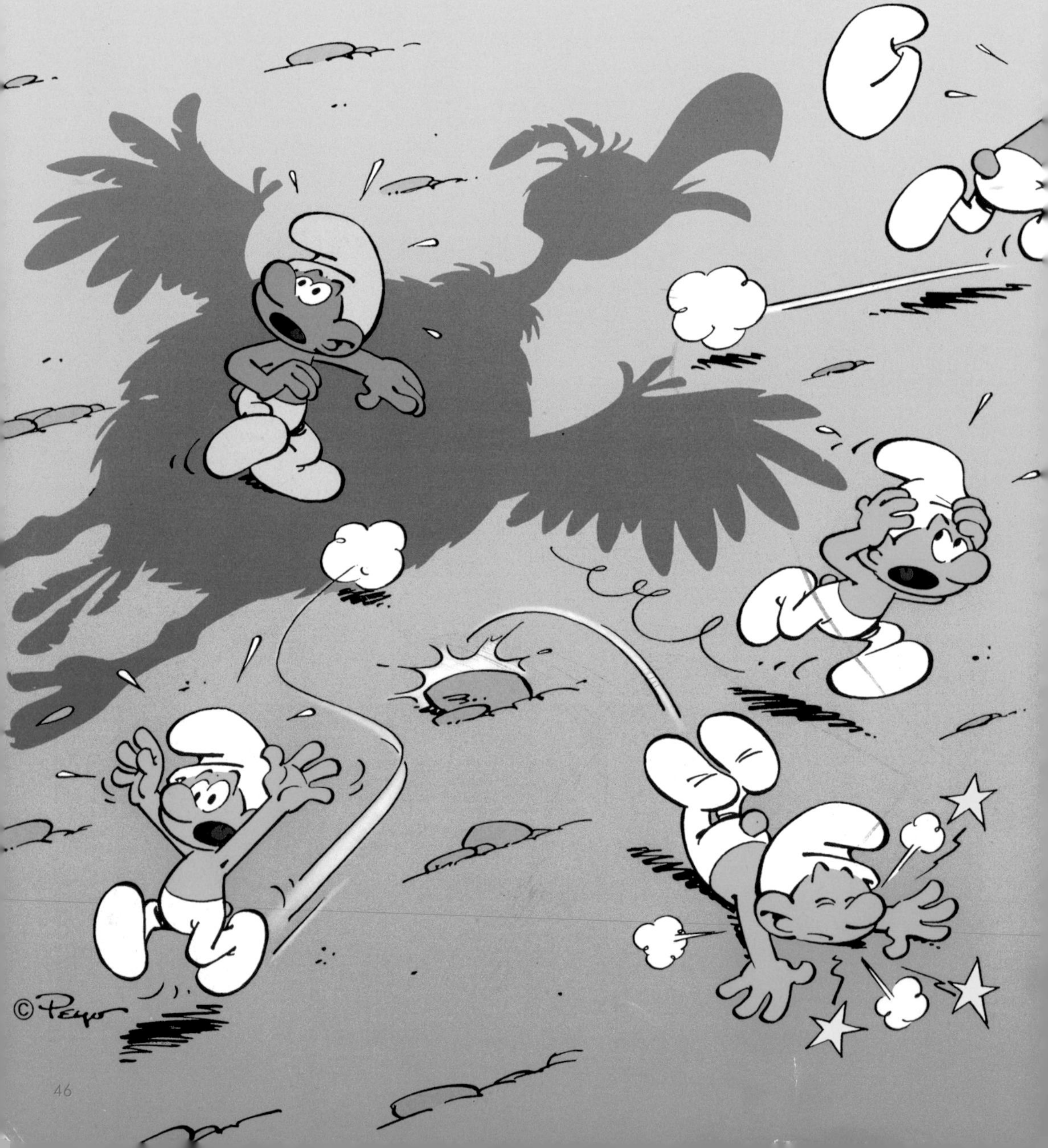
©Peyo

THE SMURFS AND THE BOOGLOOBOO

Listen to me! I saw a monster smurfing over the forest!

Oh, you must have seen a bat, Dopey Smurf! You should smurf to bed, it's late!

Uh, I'll accompany you to protect you, Smurfette! You never know!

Goodnight, Brainy Smurf! I hope you're not afraid of bats, too!

Uh...

≈Whew!≈... Smurfette was right: they're just harmless bats! Dopey Smurf scared me with his talk of monsters!

BOOGLOOBOO
BOOGLOOBOO
FLAP
FLAP FLAP
!

FLAP FLAP FLAP BOO GLOO

HELP! A monster! A flying smurf!

HEY! Who's shouting? What's smurfing?

BOO GLOO BOO

GRAACK
!

My smurf's roof has been smashed! Who... who did that?

BOOGLOOBOO
DOINC

It's the flying smurf that landed on it! It's smurfing there towards the forest!

47

Look at those foot prints, Papa Smurf!

Hmm! There's no doubt about it, they're a bird's smurfs, but it's **ENORMOUS!**

It's an exotic bird that wandered astray during its winter migration. It's no doubt smurfing its way. Go on back to smurf, there's no further danger!

Are... are you sure?

That bird was smurfing towards the southern star! It won't smurf backwards!

Towards the south? Then it's heading towards Gargamel!

FLAP FLAP FLAP FLAP FLAP FLAP FLAP

ZZz...

Later...

ZZz...

BOOGLOO BOO !

BOOGLOOBOO

BOOGLO BOO

BOOGLO BOO

!

OOGLOOOOGLOO OOGLOO

BOOK

My chimney's not a nest! Go away, you feathered beast!

© Peyo

Ah! It understood and it's leaving!

Since I'm up, I'll use the time to chop a few logs!

BOOGLOOBOO BOOGLOO BOO

?

FLAP FLAP FLAP FLAP

It's coming back with branches and leaves...

!?

BOOGLOO BOOGLOO

BOOGLOOBOO BOOGLOOO

By Beelzebub, that fiendish fowl is building a nest on my chimney!

SCAT, you overgrown chicken!

BOOGLOO

BOP

WHAM

HELP!

BOOGLOOBOO BOOGLOOBOO

FLAP FLAP FLAP

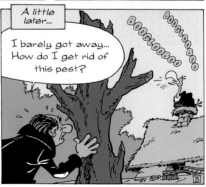

A little later...

I barely got away... How do I get rid of this pest?

BOOGLOOBOO BOOGLOOBOO

49

That afternoon...

Ah, it's leaving its nest! Now's my chance...!

I'll demolish it all! Then I'll start a fire in the chimney! That wretched bird won't ever come back! Ha ha!

What?! There's an egg in this nest!

!

BOOGLOOBEE BOOGLOOBEE

Gulp!

BOOGLOOBOO BOOGLOOBEE BOOGLOOBEE

OW! LET ME GO!

AAAAA!

Just great! I get it: the mother's telling me to keep away from her baby! Getting rid of them won't be easy!

OOGLOO

BOOGH

BOOGLOO BEEH

NIBBLE NIBBLE CHOMP

She feeds snakes to her baby! Yuck!

CHOMP MUNCH BOOGLOO MHAM! BOOGLOO BOOGLOOBOO

© Peyo

4

50

Yes, I swear to you I heard the Booglooboo's cry this morning, near the snake pond!

That can't be. Papa Smurf said that migratory smurfs smurfed towards the south and never went backwards--

BOOGLOO BOO

There! It sounds like it's coming from Gargamel's home!

You see-- I was right!

BOOGLOO FLAP FLAP FLAP FLAP FLAP FLAP

There's a baby! The mother's smurfing the nest!

Watch out! Gargamel's smurfing behind that wall!

BOOGLEEEEE

Heh heh heh!

Ha! Ha! Now I've got you! I'm going to get rid of you and your mama too!

BOOGLOOOU!!!

I'll dump you in the forest! Your mama won't ever find you and will leave my house! Heh heh heh!

He smurfed the baby into a sack!

BOOGLOO DEEEE!

After them! We must smurf the baby!

That's not safe and-- Wait for me!

BYE-BYE, BIRDIE!

VOOM

NO!

SPLOOSH

You're safe, Baby Booglooboo!

Calm down! Don't be afraid!

© Peyo

6

GLOOBEEEE SNAP
EEEEEEE!

Our friend has smurfed your life!

He-- he saw the snake that was threatening me!

NIQUE CHOMP

He's so sweet and so smurf! We could keep him!

Oh, no, we must smurf him to his mother, who's surely worried about his disappearance!

BOOGL' O BIIIII!!

At that moment...

Heh heh! That bird-brain realizes her nest is empty! Now she should leave!

FLAP FLAP FLAP FLAP FLAP BOOGLOOOO BOOGLOO BOO

BOO HOO BOOGLOO OEEBOO GLOO BOO SNIFF SNIFF

BOO? OOGLOO BOO GLOO?!

AIE! It spotted me! It's going to get revenge! BACK OFF, BOOGLOOBOO!

BOOGLOOBEEEE

FLAP FLAP FLAP FLAP

It's-- it's carrying me towards its nest?!

FLAP FLAP FLAP

No! I'm not your baby! You're mistaken!

ARGH! It wants to brood over me! It's adopted me to replace its baby!

© Peyo

At that instant...

There! He's smurfed his mama! There's no holding him back!

BOOGLOOBEE BOOGLOOBEEE

!?!

Look, he's flying!

52

BOOGLOOBOO BOOGLEE BOOGLEE BOOGLOO BOO

Him?! But how?

They're leaving me! Even better! Good riddance!

They're going away!

Goodbye, Baby Booglooboo!

Smurfs! Now I understand! They're the ones who brought back the chick!

They're too busy waving at the birds! I'll catch them by surprise! Heh heh!

Good luck!

HAAAAA! I'VE GOT YOU, YOU CURSED VERMIN!

EEEEEEE

Go ahead and scream! Nobody will come to your rescue!

EEEEEEE

EEEEEEEE

?

BOOGLOOBEEEEE

EEEEEEEE

EEEEEEE

PECK PECK PECK

HELP!

FLAP FLAP FLAP FLAP FLAP FLAP

HEY!

Hurray! They came back to smurf us!

Thanks, little Booglooboo! You're very brave!

Let him go! His mama's flying far away smurfing Gargamel towards the mountains!

HEEBEE HEEBEE HEEBEE

© Peyo 7

53

The chick's able to smurf the great voyage of the birds with his mama!

What will they do to Gargamel?

LET ME GO, YOU BIG TURKEY!

NO! DON'T LET GO OF ME... I

BOOF

EAGLES! They don't look too happy!

AHHH

He's going home, but I have an idea for... Listen... ≥whisper≤!

What an infernal day!

Hee hee! Great idea! Let's go smurf the others!

Aah! What a pleasure to be home, in peace, after all those unhappy misadventures!

BOOGLOOBOO BOOGLOOBOO BOOGLOO BOO

!

BOOGLOOBOO GLOO BOOGLOO BOO BOOGLOOBOO GLOOBOO BOOGLOO BOO BOOGLOO BOO

NOOOOO! The nightmare's starting again! MERCY!

Good idea, those bird whistles! They smurf as well as a Boogalooboo!

I wonder if we'll ever see them again?

THE END

© Peyo

WATCH OUT FOR PAPERCUTZ™

Welcome to the forever-young fifteenth SMURFS graphic novel by Peyo from Papercutz, the little company dedicated to publishing great graphic novels for all ages. I'm Jim Salicrup, the Smurf-in-Chief, with another exciting Peyo-related announcement.

As I'm sure you'll recall from THE SMURFS #14 "The Baby Smurf," we talked about 2013 shaping up as quite possibly the Smurfiest year ever! What with the all-new SMURFS 2 movie from Sony Pictures Animation, coming to a theater near you July 2013, as well as BENNY BREAKIRON, a new Papercutz graphic novel series, created by Peyo, featuring the fun-filled adventures of a super-powered little French boy, that's available now at your favorite booksellers. And the BIG NEWS this time around is that Papercutz will be publishing another new Peyo series—THE SMURFS ANTHOLOGY!

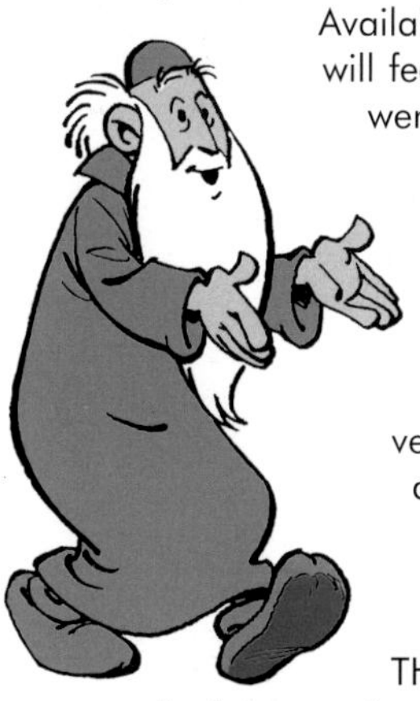

Available in deluxe hardcover editions,THE SMURFS ANTHOLOGY will feature all the original Peyo Smurfs comics, in the order they were originally published in Europe. But that's not all— each 192-page volume of THE SMURFS ANTHOLOGY will also feature the JOHAN AND PEEWIT comics, in which the Smurfs originally appeared. You remember Johan and Peewit from THE SMURFS #2 "The Smurfs and the Magic Flute," right? That's where we also met Homnibus the Enchanter, who's back for a cameo appearance in this very volume. Well, there were a few more Johan and Peewit adventures that guest-starred the Smurfs, that haven't been published before by Papercutz, so these comics will be collected exclusively in THE SMURFS ANTHOLOGY. Coming in June 2013, we're sure no Blue-Believer will want to miss THE SMURFS ANTHOLOGY.

In the meantime, the Smurfiness continues here too! Coming soon is THE SMURFS #16 "The Aerosmurf," the long-awaited sequel to "The Flying Smurf" story that appeared in THE SMURFS #1 "The Purple Smurfs." Finally, the Smurf who dreamed of flying finally gets his wish—but when his flying somehow results in Smurfette getting captured by Gargamel, it's up to him to rescue her!

Yes, 2013 is truly a very Smurfy year!
Smurf you later!

Jim

STAY IN TOUCH!
EMAIL: Salicrup@papercutz.com
WEB: www.papercutz.com
TWITTER: @papercutzgn
FACEBOOK: PAPERCUTZGRAPHICNOVELS
SNAIL MAIL: Papercutz, 160 Broadway, Suite 700, East Wing, New York, NY 10038

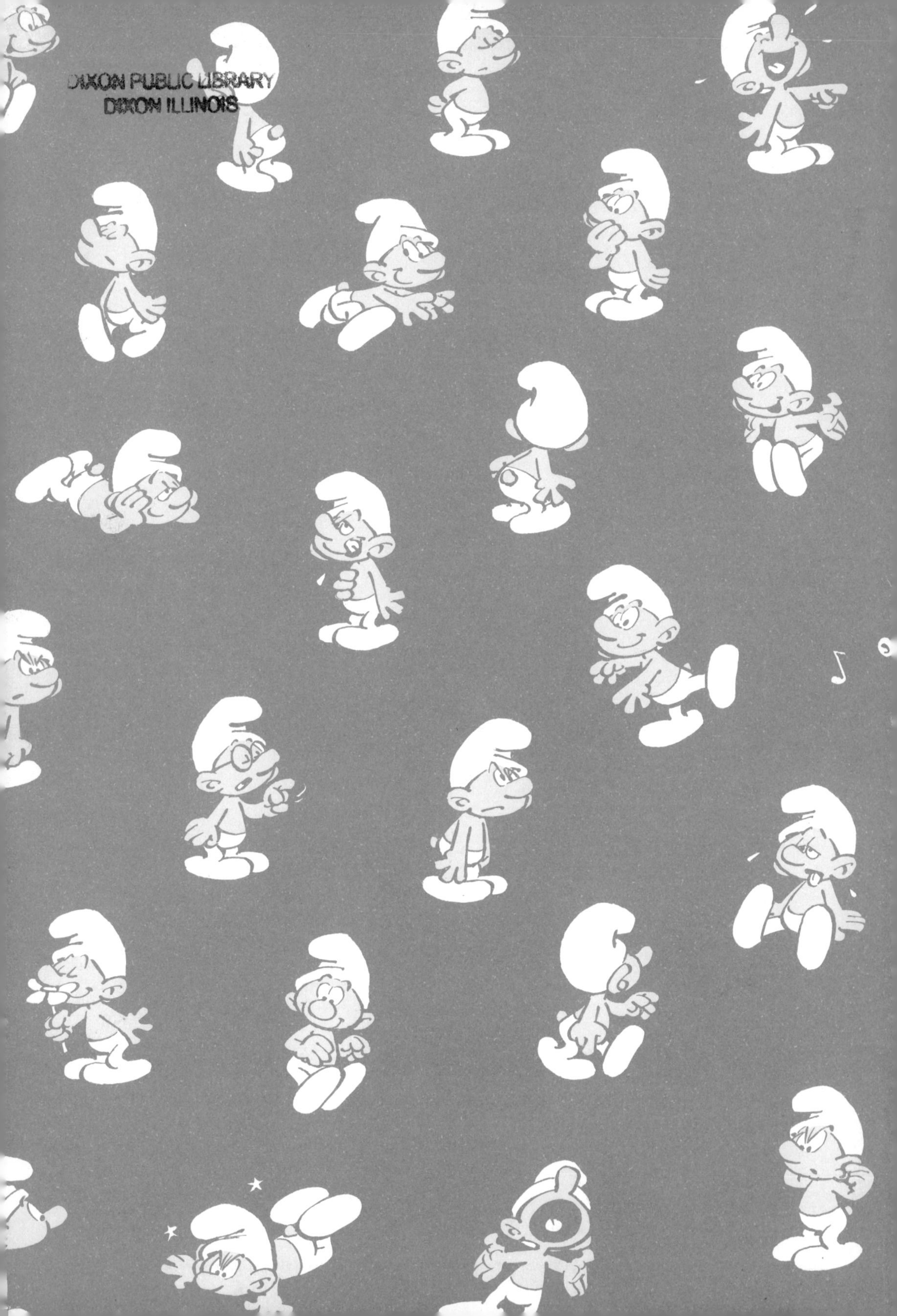